I AM NOT A FILM STAR

Crime Thriller Novel

Vinod Narayanan

NYNA BOOKS
www.nynabooks.com

English Language
I am not a film star
(Crime Thriller Novel)

Vinod Narayanan
Rights Reserved

First print Edition: May 2022

ISBN: 9798831516692

Cover & Typesetting: Boons Entertainments

Published by
NYNA BOOKS
MSME/UAN Regd. KL07D0004957
www.nynabooks.com
Email: **nynabooks@gmail.com**

Warning

This novel is for adults only. Each of the characters has a definite personality. So their thoughts, conversations and actions are theirs alone. The narrator has nothing to do with it.

The story and characters are purely fictional. The novel has nothing to do with existing individuals, institutions, caste, religious organizations or centers of power.

The international sex market is worth billions. It is intertwined with all other illegal businesses. From drug dealing to money laundering, it's all about the sex business. This novel tells the story of such an underworld.

Chapter 1

Singapore.

Time 12 noon.

It is a multi-storey luxury mansion.

In the master bedroom in that premium apartment you can see the city of Singapore lying down.

Vehicles are moving on the road to Mandal Lake.

The multi-storey glass houses on Mandal Road shine in the sun.

The bright blue water of the Upper Pierce Reservoir was still.

Across the reservoir lies the greenery of the Bukit Thomas Nature Reserve.

Ansula rolled her eyes from the distance.

She is naked.

Makeup is applied all over the body as usual.

But it was so perfect that it didn't feel like makeup.

The duty of third-rate professionals in Hollywood.

Riding above her is a Negro.

His quoted organ made her scare her but it didn't hurt.

Probably the strength of the amphetamine.

"Be Conscious Lady."

The reprimand was heard.

The voice is by Sandeep Kulkarni.

He is the director of that Porn movie.

The scene is shot live by three cameras from three angles.

Three cameramen, a make - up artist, two light controllers, director Sandeep Kulkarni and cinematography director Elizabeth.

Elizabeth is a California woman in her fifties.

A blonde.

"React without lying like a dead body."

Sandeep Kulkarni shouted again.

Ansula responded automatically.

"I think the drug is overdosed. She is half unconscious. "

"Okay. Then they take a next position. Off all camera and play on add. "

Sandeep was dissatisfied and instructed to go to the editing room through intercom.

Then he said to the Negro:

"Pedra, please take a next position. You can screw her ass. "

"Okay."

Pedra rose from the top of Ansula.

His elongated organ fluttered in the air.

Sandeep Kulkarni was sitting next to Ansula.

She tried to get up.

She went into a trance like an alcoholic.

"Kneel down and lie down."

Sandeep Kulkarni suggested to her.

"Then no one will recognize that your face is mechanical and semi-conscious."

Ansula knelt on the bed, leaned forward, hugged the pillow and lay down.

Elizabeth helped them make that pose.

Ansula's buttocks stretched out.

The makeup artist touched and enchanted that part.

The protruding petals turned red.

Bleeding color spread to the ankles and thighs.

Sandeep Kulkarni pressed her buttocks and got up from the bed.

He suggested.

"Lights on. Starts all camera … and action. "

Elizabeth applied jelly to Pedra's long organ.

It became stronger as her hands moved smoothly.

She kissed it eagerly and pulled away.

Pedra climbed into bed.

He stood behind Ansula like a bull and pushed his organ into her ass area.

He put it completely inside her and he reached out with both hands and rubbed her nipples.

In Ansula's half-consciousness, her new empire, her husband, her baby, her community, Laila, Sandeep Kulkarni … and the luxury bed in her frozen room in Singapore were all circling like a movie.

She is been two months since the rise of a Porn star.

Ansula's last duty as a journalist was through the sting operation of the Malayalam news channel News plus Seventeen.

The sting operation was aimed at cracking down on a sex racket that had spread a net in the metro city of Kochi.

Sandeep Kulkarni, who pretended to be a customer, caught Ansula in the hotel room dressed as a prostitute with hidden cameras.

He turned it into an exclusive program for the English Channel World Big C News.

It was only later that Ansula realized the truth.

Sandeep Kulkarni owns both the television channels.

His wife is her madam who leads News plus Seventeen.

Her best friend and channel colleague Laila is Sandeep's main right hand man.

But he did not disappoint her.

Gave promotion.

He injected her with cocaine and made her naked after sedating her.

He put on makeup all over his body and played with a porn star on the bed of a luxury van and showed it to the whole world live.

Through Sandeep Kulkarni's online video channel Dodo Porn.

The channel's rating skyrocketed.

The world liked the live broadcast of a Malayalee woman's beauty and sexual misconduct.

So Ansula became a star in a day.

Sandeep did not show any reduction for her remuneration.

He was a perfect professional at that matter.

At present, Ansula is paid Rs 35 lakh per sitting.

Twelve crore rupees in two months.

She settled in Singapore with husband and baby.

Ratheesh's husband is proud that his wife is Porn star but Malayalees are like that he doesn't have to take it.

Ratheesh now has to say that there is a moral police stick in every malayalees. So he locked his current Face book account.

It was directed by Ratheesh KG. It was called Ambati. It was locked when the Pongala of the moral police started coming. Malayalees is like that. They enjoyed everything about Ansula through dodo porn.

With limited access to video downloads on Dodo porn, Anzula's mobile phone camera was left open in front of his laptop and he enjoyed sharing video clips on WhatsApp.

Her thighs, breasts and buttocks were seen in HD visuals.

Even Ratheesh celebrated the discovery of Mallus in HD Clarity, even the twin's mark of Ansula's private parts that he had never seen before.

Then they repeatedly masturbated.

Not content with that, they went to look at the bathrooms and bedrooms of Shoshamma or Faisala in the neighborhood.

After that they all became moral police.

Ratheesh got angry and created a Face book ID.

Dimora Thefe.

In it, Mark Zuckerberg's cousin takes a picture of Allen Mario and turns it into a profile picture.

One mallus' front request was neither taken nor given.

The face book fan page of Ansula was renamed Ansula Dimora.

He then posted photo poses covering Ansula's nipples and sweet pussy and loaded the person on the dodo phone.

Nipples and sweet pussy are against Face book's privacy policy.

So all the birds in the world except humans are against Face book's privacy policy.

How a goat hides his genitals.

Can a cow follow a privacy policy?

Not at all about an elephant.

A tremor can sometimes embarrass everyone.

That's how Ratheesh's thought.

So he took a picture of Zuckerberg's cousin's profile picture and gave it to face book.

Pedro was constantly moving behind Ansula.

Sometimes he moved automatically and other times he moved faster.

In that position he began to have sex.

It's been more than half an hour.

It is the force of an injection taken into his organ.

It prolongs orgasm and works like a machine without any loss of strength.

Sandeep Kulkarni and the cameramen got bored as it was a regular sight.

When he got tired, Sandeep Kulkarni called

"Pedro, put in her mouth."

As soon as Pedro heard this, he pulled the weapon from Ansula's buttocks and inserted it into her mouth.

It felt completely different and warm to Pedro.

He closed his eyes and nodded.

The heat of his mouth, the gnashing of his teeth and the movement of his tongue quickly led him to ecstasy.

Soon he had ejaculated in her mouth.

It unusually covered her entire face like an ice cream year.

"Cut."

The cameras are off.

The lights went out.

Chapter 2

'Anshula Dimora Rise of a Porn star!'

That was the title of the photo feature written by Kochi bureau chief and special correspondent Marthandan in the Sunday supplement of the Malayalam daily.

While the sex rackets that drain the spirit, mind and wealth of the youth are spreading money over the metro city of Kochi, those who wander in power are turning to stone with the scent of sex.

A caption column with white letters in a pink column.

Anshula Dimora's photo feature also highlights issues such as the entry of women into Sabarimala, the raffle deal, Israel's rocket fire on the Palestinian people, and the government's women's wall.

From the photo of the trainee journalist, who was paid Rs 8,000, to the Porn star look with make-up all over her body, Ansula's photos were printed in the newspaper.

In just two months, Ansula's husband and baby settled in Singapore, having grown to a salary of over Rs 1 crore per sitting.

Dodo is the most expensive player to raise the rating of Porn channel.

But the feature does not reveal who owns the Dodo phone channel or what his connection is with World Big C News and the Malayalam news channel News plus Seventeen. Despite being a fierce rival, the Malayalam view deliberately hid it out of love for its media colleagues.

Yesterday, that is, Saturday night, Marthandan achieved what he had long wanted.

Sub-editor Jesimole got his hands.

Jesse wanted it too.

Marthandan and Jesse worked alone in that one - room bureau office during the day.

Occasional advertisers and frequent walkers through the verandah forbade their sexual desires.

Ansula Dimora's change to a star from Ansula Ratheesh, a junior TV channel reporter who lived in Panampilly Nagar, Kochi two months ago, was ordered to make a story by chief editor Mammen Thomas.

The story should be made on Saturday itself.

Must arrive at the head office no later than 9 p.m.

The printing of the Sunday Supplement should be completed before two o'clock at night.

Therefore, the Kochi bureau office of Malayalamkazha must be functioning on Saturday night.

Marthandan kept the spice food parcels and water bottles in advance.

The main story was written by Marthandan.

The sub-features were written and prepared by Jesse.

Features went to the head office via email, including DTP at 9:30 and photos collected from the net and obtained from a private source.

Then, with a sigh, Martahandan straightened his legs and looked at Jessy.

"It's half past nine."

Jesse said looking at his gaze.

"Can We Protect the Moral Value of the City of Arabian Sea?"

"Shit ... you eat that spicy Dosa and spread your legs girl"

Jessy look him.

She got up, went to the small washbasin at the back of the room, washed her hands and unpacked the food parcels from Hotel Aryas.

The masala dosas, wrapped in plastic wrap, were frozen.

The chutney and sambar were unwrapped from the covers and shaken into the dosa.

"I called home and told them."

Jesse said as he ate the dosa.

Marthandon asked, eating with her.

"What?"

"Night"

"This night office your family should see."

"It doesn't matter ... I'm not a believer, but I'm a staff member of a corporate newspaper."

"That's good. Faith is everything. ”

With that, Marthanda reached out and held her breasts.

Strong big breasts.

Jesse said tapping that hand.

"Eat the Dosa."

After the meal, Marthandan made a bed by the tables and spreading the old Malayalam newspapers on the floor.

The shutters on the outside were closed from the inside as soon as the evening meal was brought.

Otherwise the veranda will be full of harassment by the moral police.

This is the norm for any man who has to work with a single lady staff.

Marthandon turned off the lights.

Jesse stood in the dark.

The light from the outside streetlight enters through the window panes.

Marthandan sat behind her.

His waist rested on her plump buttocks.

She stopped as his hands began to rub her breasts.

"Stop... dress will be bad."

Her black churidar was full of gilt embellishments.

Marthandon said in his mind that Jesse's white body was beautiful in that black dress.

She undressed and he undressed too.

When she took off her bra, he realized the naked truth.

It was a padded bra.

"It was to this padded bra that I showed my strength?"

Marthandon said in frustration

"Burning truths ..."

Jesse joked and laughed.

He stroked her small breasts.

"Small and beautiful."

He ran his hands down her body.

She ran her fingers through her panties.

The place was completely wet.

"Oh my princess ..."

He said and gently bit her ear.

Then he put his lips on her nipples and sucked.

They were down, but the ridges were rising.

They are thick and large.

He put her on the table and took off her panties.

She spread her white fat thighs.

He buried his face into her wet romance.

Everything that Jesse contained was shattered.

Jesse felt Marthandon's lips sticking to the throbbing lips of an animal crawling under her abdomen.

Jesse laughed in the dark when he remembered that the man he always respectfully called Sir was showing on her secret area with his lips.

She wanted to laugh out loud.

But environmental awareness did not allow it.

Instead it came out as a big scream.

She rubbed her nipples with her own hands.

She twisted her ankles and put them on Marthandan's outside and tightened her grip on him.

Marthandan now realizes that Jessie is so strong.

She glowed like a passing stream.

She continued to squirm, releasing the scream.

The next moment a strong fountain of cream from her secret lake fell on the face and mouth of the Kochi bureau chief.

When he changed his face, she gripped his hair tightly and moved his face into her secret area.

It kept dripping with water until it stopped licking its lips.

Until then she pressed his face to hers.

When it was all over, she let out a deep sigh, untied her ankles, pushed him on his shoulder with her legs and pushed him back.

Marthandan thought she was treating him like a dog.

She is his junior, and he always calls her Sir.

I am the boss in this office.

Is it polite of her to treat me like this?

What is she doing?

He sat on the ground and thought.

He tore the India Today page and wiped Jesse's secret liquid off his face.

The genital fluid of an ordinary lady is on the face of a special correspondent of a leading newspaper.

He looked up at the table.

Jesse puts her hands behind her back and sits lazily on the table.

That pose could have been a poster for an A movie.

Marthandan thought he had not used his weapon.

He jumped up.

He stood up between her thighs and hugged her tightly.

He pressed his lips together and kissed her.

His weapon also kissed her secret garden.

He picked her up and slid her into the Malayalam daily spread out below.

He slowly entered through her wide thighs.

He was surprised when he injected her with no defenses.

"Aren't you virgin?"

He asked as he moved.

"Not ripe."

She brought the seal.

"Who broke the seal?"

"Sir Muraleedharan on City Cable TV."

"What was your job there?"

"Newsreader ... Stayed there for a year. Then he entered Malayalam daily.

"Is Muraleedharan still being playing you, dear?"

"No ... His wife picked it up. That's when my work was gone. It was good fun there. The newsreader's popularity is not here...there were three lakh viewers ..."

"Why?"

"Why .... To see my news ..."

"I thought he would have shot it and put it on YouTube ..."

"Well ... that event will not cost me anything ... You will see Jesse the original person ..."

"God...no...No ..."

Marthandan swore during the quick movement...

Jesse's breathing slowed.

Marthandan increased the speed of his movement as he changed gears of the vehicle.

Chapter 3

It was past midnight on Saturday.

In the middle of Malaysia, a black car came and stopped under a veil of darkness under a huge apartment building in the city center.

Many CCTV cameras did not capture it because it was located among a row of coniferous trees.

The two men got out of the car and jumped on top of the van like circus performers.

From there it quickly climbed to the top of the wall.

From there it quickly climbed up through the building's pipeline.

Their journey was as fast as you can see in some movies.

Clinging like an iguana, they climbed to the top at the speed of a cobra.

When they reached the 21st floor, they hid on the balcony at dawn.

There were two settees lying there.

A laptop was left open on top of the teapot.

There was a movie playing in it.

That too is a porn film.

The porn film stars Emma Nickinson playing with two men.

The two strangers looked at each other.

One stranger looked inside.

The light from the chandelier is scattered inside.

A man faints in bed.

A bottle of Old Tom Gin is on the table.

A cup is overturned.

The two strangers slowly entered.

One of them picked up the jinn's bottle, sniffed it and put it back.

They moved to the next room.

There is a dim light.

A three-year-old baby is lying in bed.

It's in deep sleep.

The unidentified man slowly picked up the baby and put it in his backpack.

Then he looked at the other.

Without wasting any time, they quickly descended as soon as they came out of the room.

The van with the baby sped through the darkness.

Chapter 4

It was Sunday.

In the pale yellow sun, the skyscrapers of the city were painted yellow.

The city is getting busier.

The 21st floor apartment in the Goljan Leaf apartment complex belongs to Ansula.

She is in Kuwait for the shooting.

It's been two days.

Ratheesh woke up.

The mobile keeps ringing non-stop.

Ratheesh picked up the phone.

Not Ansula.

He answered the call with suspicion.

"Good morning dear."

The male voice of majestic signature.

English has an American slang.

"I Have Something to Tell You"

"Yes tell me."

"Ansulas husband must listen this talk."

Suddenly he heard a baby crying on the other end of the phone in the pure Malayalam.

"Dad,"

"Hey Naomi ... daughter ...?"

Ratheesh panicked and ran to the boy's bedroom.

The baby is not there.

He put the phone to his ear and searched the entire apartment.

"You cannot find the kid there because he's here with us."

"Why Did You Kidnap My Kid?"

"This is not your child."

"What nonsense are you talking about?"

"Yes. This is the child of the Great Ansula"

"What is your need?"

"We have two requirements. First of all, you have to pay us Rs 10 crore. "

"My God, Rs 10 crore?"

"Listen to the second demand. Ansula Dimora should quit her job as Porn star. She should never be in front of the camera again. "

"Who are you?"

"Aren't you her husband?" How many people are fucking her? That too became public in the eyes of the world. She's satisfied with their long penis and she's despising your little black penis. "

"Shut up. You do not know if I have a wound on my mind. So do not try to magnify it. "

"You are a shameless husband. A parasite that eats with the money that his wife play sex from a stranger. "

"Stop it Bloody Bastard."

Ratheesh yelled.

He lost all control.

He can hear a gentle laugh from the other side.

Again the stranger began to speak.

"Hey ... listen to what I say. Do not be so ashamed. You consult together. Those two twin spots on your wife's vagina are now familiar all over the world. Do you know how many people are discussing it? You can clearly see how her secret organ trembles abnormally during orgasm. I have a big screen in my house. That too in HD."

He continued laughing.

Ratheesh threw the phone to the floor with force as it was beyond tolerable.

It was scattered into many pieces.

Ratheesh felt as if a large pebble had been placed on top of his chest.

This is how people think.

This world is making fun of me God...

The next moment he was filled with anger

"Paranaris who moan and mock themselves after seeing Ansula Dimora's naked and enjoying themselves."

With that single sentence, he suppressed all the ridicule of the world and fell on the sofa.

Tears flowed from her eyes.

It is a clash between morality and sexual freedom.

The human body is just a mass of flesh that rots when life is lost.

What makes each of its organs unique?

A sensation obtained when the organs of a man and a woman are joined together.

The feeling that others get when they see it.

How can this be wrong?

How can you determine if that experience and that organ are the private property of a particular partner?

What is the moral of it?

So who is Ansula himself?

She's not someone else's

Doesn't Sandeep Kulkarni now have more power and authority over her body than he does? Thus the contract is also signed.

But the money she earns ... isn't that mine too...our daughter Naomi, isn't she mine...

When Naomi came to his senses, Ratheesh regained consciousness.

He jumped up.

He snatched the SIM card from the wreckage of the broken phone on the floor and put it in another phone.

But the kidnappers could not find the number called by the kidnappers.

Call history was unavailable because the phone is different.

He called Ansula's phone.

No one took it except it rang for a while

Ansula has a nanny.

Nicky is of African descent

But she is Sandeep's fellow.

She does not pick up his phone so as not to interrupt the shoot.

Ratheesh called Ansula's phone at least five times.

There is no escape.

He called Sandeep Kulkarni's number.

At first he did not pick up but when he kept calling, Sandeep Kulkarni picked up the phone and asked angrily

"What do you want Ratheesh ..."

"Someone kidnapped the child."

"What?"

"Someone abducted my daughter Naomi."

"When?"

"It simply came to our notice then. The baby was in the bedroom until I fell asleep at night. The time is not morning. A while ago someone called and threatened and said he was kidnapped. Ten crore should be given. Ansula should stop acting in porn movies. This is what they needed. ”

"Have you asked who this game is for?"

"I did not ask."

"And...Angelo toy...she is behind this ..."

“Who is that?"

"It's a super porn film star. With the arrival of Insular, the crown was thrown. Was the eternal presence of Dodo porn? Now she is into locked in the real life porn movie. ”

"Real life porn movie...what is that?"

"It simply came to our notice then. Real life porn channels are the channels that hijack CCTV cameras in the rooms of houses with women and show live footage of them. Gentle young women do not even dream that the whole world is watching what they are doing. It does not need CCTV cameras. The webcam on the laptop and the camera on the mobile can all be hijacked and leaked live without the owner knowing. Scenes from the homes, bedrooms, bathrooms and other private spaces of every home are being watched live around the world. If we want to see it too, all we have to do is go to that channel, pay and subscribe. Some people act like this with some porn stars. For example real life porn shows like the Big Boss TV show. The audience can decide which houses to choose. Angelo Toy is currently doing such shows. Your child was abducted by her men. ”

"What to do?"

“Let me see. Ansula should not know this information. Tension will affect the shoot. ”

After saying that, Sandeep Kulkarni hung up the phone.

"Idiot."

Sandeep said angrily.

His manager Peter Hobbit and Ansula's nickname were standing nearby.

He spoke to them in a low voice.

"Ansula's child Naomi has been abducted by Angelo Toy's men. Ansula should not know this information for any reason. Be Careful. It will affect the film. ”

"She caught a new track."

Manager Peter Hobbit said.

"What...isn't it a real porn life show...isn't it because of misbehavior ... she called us bad"?

Sandeep Kulkarni scoffed.

"No, sir. She moved to Porn Village in Atlantis Valley, rented a studio and began filmmaking. Porn movies. A one - and - a - half hour movie costs just $ 15,000. Every setup is ready there. ”

"My God"

Sandeep was surprised.

“It could be released on Amazon Prime and Netflix. Video can be sold on demand via Vimeo and the clip will go through YouTube and Porn tube. Profit in any way. In addition, Sri Lanka, India, Maldives and South African countries can run fillers in C-class theaters here. Money will come and go. This is the business of the Porn villages in the Atlantis Valley. There are about a hundred studios in the group. Jobs for everyone. No government rules apply to them. ”

“If we start one too. What can be done with this Ansula. The nicknamed action heroine, the forest dweller, the nun...Huge Rolls... and we can also act with this Nikki. ”

Laughing at that, he reached under Nicky's mini skirt and squeezed the top of her panties.

Nikki burst out laughing.

This time the gymnasium set was placed on the shooting floor.

Chapter 5

It's just dawn.

The eastern dimension is becoming clearer.

Laila thoughtfully stood on the small balcony of her flat in Kadavanthara, Kochi the metro city of Kerala.

Below you can see the whole city.

You can see the chimney of the Cochin refinery burning in the far southeast.

It is Sunday.

Laila has a newspaper in her hand.

Ansula's story in the Malayalam daily's Sunday supplement was hot.

"Ansula Dimora ... The Rise of a Porn star!"

Special Correspondent Marthandan.

It's a work in progress.

Marthandan himself leaked the information.

To settle the feud with Sandeep Kulkarni, Madam and Ansula.

He has collaborated with Sandeep and Madam for whatever purpose.

Ansula has become a star by throwing herself like a curry leaf.

Not that his body was a little fat.

Doesn't she deserve to be a porn star?

Sandeep is amazed at Ansula's beauty.

The nudity of a woman who is completely Malayalam is in great demand in the Porn market.

On Laila's buttocks, something warm touched the top of her light night gown.

Warm of breath in the back of the neck.

Laila understood.

She turned around and whispered.

"Noah?"

"When did you come last night? Can't I see you now? "

Noah said in a trembling voice.

That voice was shaken by excessive lust or grief.

Laila turned and stood.

Then his organ hit her abdomen.

She looked down with a smirk.

It's exciting.

She said with a perfect smirk

"It simply came to our notice then. Do you want to make my clothes dirty? "

"Laila ... Please"

"Leave me alone"

"Don't insult me Laila."

Noah was on the verge of tears.

Laila wondered if her husband was unusually crazy.

She reached out and touched it.

Now it will be excreted and exhausted.

She hugged it.

It just got bigger.

Laila was shocked.

She looked around.

Anyone can see this scene with a binocular or a zoom lens camera.

She grabbed Noah and put him on the set in the living room.

He was completely naked.

She knelt in front of him and then she took his quoted organ in her mouth and started licking.

Noah let out a sigh of relief.

In the four years since the wedding, Laila has not seen it so big.

Moreover, it has the nature of excreting as soon as she touches it.

It's been licking Laila's mouth for about half an hour.

Laila was surprised.

Noah traveled through the heights of bliss.

Laila stood up, took off her nightgown, spread her legs and went to Noah's lap.

She was quoting the full quote and sitting back inside

It took refuge in her warmth.

After a long time, Noah knew the heat of his wife's flesh.

She began to rise and fall on top of him.

Her wide breasts were dripping.

Noah held them in his hands and stroked the nipples with his fingertips.

Laila closed her eyes as if on a ride through the golden clouds.

She did not take any performance drugs because it was early in the morning and unexpected.

In the case of Noah, it is generally not necessary.

But what is happening now.

Laila enters the sharpness of the first time unintentionally and enters the second time like a storm.

It's like a wave crawling under the abdomen.

At the same time, Noah let out a stream of hot air.

Laila hugged Noah until the waves stopped.

Then the mobile rang.

Laila pulled away from Noah, got up from her lap and looked at her mobile.

Ansula's husband is Ratheesh.

Did you see the newspaper and call to say something bad?

How does he know this information?

Anyway Laila answered the phone.

"Hi Ratheesh!"

"Aren't you feeling well in Kochi?"

Ratheesh's voice sounded muffled.

Laila became as innocent as if she knew nothing

"Allah ... I am scared to stay in Kochi now ... The latest news is that there was a shooting at the beauty parlor of film actress Jennifer in broad daylight. They are the goons of Shiva Pandari who are shaking the Mumbai underworld. She is my friend. A fraud. She's likely to be the one who signed it. ”

"Get rid of it all ... I have something to say ... and then I need to know something."

"Say ..."

Laila smelled danger and became alert.

"It simply came to our notice then. I saw the feature about Ansula in their online version in today's Malayalam view. It includes our personal lives. It's up to you. But the channel did not utter a single word about the gentlemen. These media dogs have a great desire to attack when they are alone. How did that leak, Laila? ”

Laila think about the channel head Madam and Madam's husband Sandeep Kulkrney. If Ratheesh records this conversation and listens to Kulkarni, her story will end.

So her instincts advised her to stick to the policy.

"What a Ratheesh, talking like a country girl. What sources do journalists have? For example, our police do not know where Sukumara Kurup is, but the journalists here know. That is their network. But Ratheesh, you know what the hype this feature would be for Ansula. Now all men will Google and type Ansula Dimora. Visitors gather at Dodo Pony. Thanks to Ansula, they will get more subscribers. With that, Ansula's career graph will go up. "

"Fuck ... how I can look at my own country, among my friends, at the faces of my own people, at the face of my own mother. Can I still come to Kerala? "

Ratheesh broke his words.

He cried.

Laila did not say anything.

Ratheesh continued.

"When my daughter grows up ... oh ... yes I called to say that. Naomi was abducted last night. "

"What ... who is kidnap Naomi?"

"It simply came to our notice then. When I woke up in the morning there was no baby in bed. Also a phone call came. Their demand is for Rs 10 crore to get the child back. Also, Ansula should stop acting in Porn movies. That is their demand. I do not know. I called Sandeep Kulkarni and told him the information. He says it was done by actress Angela Toy. Their stardom is the antithesis of Ansula's abduction. "

"O Allah."

Laila was overjoyed but she acted anxious.

Ratheesh continued.

"Can I trust Sandeep Kulkarni? Do you know them all well, Laila? Is there any benefit? "

"Don't be afraid Ratheesh. Sandeep will handle it beautifully. He has goons and quoting gangs. "

"Then one thing Laila. Sandeep Kulkarni has specifically told Ansula not to know this. Don't say that when you call her. "

"No, she's not aware of this for the time being."

Laila said.

On the other hand, Ratheesh hung up the phone.

Laila's heart swelled with joy.

"How fast Allah gives work to my adversaries."

She personally dialed the number of the Malayalam daily's Special Correspondent Marthandan on her mobile.

Chapter 6

That Sunday morning, Marthandan took Jesimole to the Kaloor bus stand, put her on a bus and returned home.

He slept through the whole day.

In one night, Jesimol became Marthandon's Big Boss.

Marthandan felt comfortable listening to what she had to say.

Thick thighs and strong small breasts.

Is that Jesse's plus point?

Or the length of time?

Or her mockery of his manhood?

Laila's phone rang while Marthandan was wondering where he had gone as a little mouse in front of Jessy.

"You have exclusive news, Marthandan"

Laila started.

"Tell Laila ..."

Marthandon became anxious.

There is some give and take between reporters.

Some news that does not suit the politics and management of their media to someone else will give.

Every media is the property of every capitalist.

Then each media will have its own vested interests, personal interests, political interests and business interests. A news item comes out after filtering all this.

"Naomi, Ansula's baby, has been abducted. They are supposed to be the people of the porn star Angel Toy. "

"It simply came to our notice then. If this is breaking news in News plus Seventeen now, then there is no point in printing this news in Malayalam tomorrow. "

“No. This is not the case with News plus Seventeen. They will not give the news. ”

"But the details should be WhatsApp"

"Sure."

Laila cut off her mobile and put it on the sofa.

The semen on her thighs was dry and sticky.

That's when she remembered that she was completely naked.

She looked at Noah on the couch.

Noah just kept his mouth open.

The face is wide with joy.

Laila ran to him and shook him and called.

Noah fell on the sofa, like a withered plant…

His heartbeat was still.

Noah is dead.

Laila was shocked.

She then noticed the syringe and ampoule in the side table.

Noah was injected with a powerful amphetamine.

A sexual stimulant drug from online.

Laila lay on the floor with a scream.

Chapter 7

Marthandan's time seems clear.

Martahnden was instructed to follow the news that Ansula's baby had been abducted.

Editor-in-Chief Varghese Tharakan called Marthandan directly from Thiruvananthapuram.

The next flight is to fly to Singapore.

All the details of the Porn film mafia with roots in Kerala should be collected.

The goal is a gigantic exclusive feature.

And the news of Anzula's kidnapping will be given prominence at the countdown - until the child is found by the investigating agencies.

Marthandan thanked her heartily.

She should be treated well.

Laila meet him a year ago in connection with the arrest of the famous film actor.

The arrest of the famous actor by the police in the case of torturing the famous actress had made big news.

The entire media had to camp day and night in front of the Aluva Police Club and around the actor's house.

The actor was brought by the police and when he waited for the night hours, he went behind a boulder and thought he would faint a bit.

Laila was sleeping there at the time - for News plus Seventeen. Familiar then. Then she put her head on his lap and fell asleep.

Before they had time to tune in properly, the police brought in a prominent actor. Her cameraman came and called her too.

During his trip to Singapore for a Malayalam daily, Marthandan made only one request to chief.

He wants Jesse as his assistant.

Management was willing to do anything for Hot Story.

Sub-editor Kaduthuruthy Saji has been given temporary charge of the Kochi bureau.

It was unthinkable for him to let go Jesse with Saji.

Marthandan boarded a flight from Nedumbassery to Singapore with Jesse at 4.30 that evening.

Chapter 8

Ratheesh is upset in his apartment room in Singapore.

He drank some whiskey and lit a cigarette.

He kept calling Sandeep Kulkarni every hour of the day.

He did not pick up the phone.

There is no point in calling Ansula.

She has not received a single call today.

It was said that the shooting was in Kuwait.

Ratheesh tried Sandeep Kulkarni's number again.

Now, Sandeep picked up the phone without hesitation.

He spoke hotly.

"Ratheesh, I have 26 missed calls on my phone. Are you crazy? "

"It has been 12 hours since I lost my baby. Do you have any information? "

"My people do exactly that."

"What information?"

"I'll tell you later."

Sandeep Kulkarni said angrily.

Listening to Thai music in the background over the phone.

This is similar to what is commonly heard at Thai beach carnivals.

Will it happen in Kuwait?

Ratheesh was skeptical.

But he did not show it.

Asked instead

"Should I report it to the police?"

On the other hand, a few sighs

And then replied in a threatening tone.

"But you and your wife will go to jail. I will not be touched by anything. "

Sandeep Kulkarni hung up the phone.

Ratheesh anxiously dialed him again but was told that the phone was switched off.

Ratheesh called Ansula's helper Nikki.

No response.

He sent an SMS to Ansula's phone.

"Call Me in urgent... Naomi Is Missing."

Nikki was in possession of Ansula's bag and belongings.

The message came on Ansula's phone and she showed it to Sandeep who was watching the shooting closely.

He bought it and read it.

His face lit up with anger.

He deleted the message and turned off the phone.

Ansula is played by a Mongolian-faced man in the middle of the lights on the shooting floor.

He was a Korean.

Makeup artist Elizabeth was injecting a sexual stimulant Dragon Hover into the body of a completely naked Negro in the next table. As she looks at it, that organ has become abnormally large and strong.

Elizabeth put gel on it.

The Negro walked towards Ansula like a bull.

It was getting dark that day, but Ansula's organ could not rest.

Doubt intensified in Ratheesh's mind.

Ansula is not in Kuwait but in Thailand.

Thai music is commonly heard at Thai Beach Carnival.

In Kuwait it is never possible.

At that moment the calling bell rang.

Ratheesh was shocked.

He looked at the door camera screen.

It is a man and a woman.

It is clear at a glance that they are Malayalees.

Ratheesh opened the door.

"Who are you?"

"I'm Marthandan. Is the Special Correspondent. Laila is my friend. She was the one who told the information. This is my assistant Jesse. ”

Introduced to Marthandan.

Ratheesh invited them both inside.

"There was sad news. Did Ratheesh know?

"No. What is it? "

"Laila's husband Noah is dead. It was morning. Heart attack. "

"God. I'm called her in the morning. After seeing the Sunday supplement feature in Malayalam. I realized it was her job.

Ratheesh did not hide his anger.

Marthandan and Jesse looked at each other with a frown.

"Sorry Ratheesh. Thought it would give you hype as a professional. You know that the moral police in our society do not approve of praising a Porn star directly. "

"It's alright ... you sit-down."

"I knew the baby had been abducted."

"Laila must have said ... hot news."

"Yes...do you have any information?"

"No information."

"Didn't you inform the police?"

"No. Sandeep Kulkarni does not agree with that. He is threatening Ansula and I are to go jail if we complain to the police. He further added that Naomi was abducted by Angela Toy, a porn film star in the area. He says he can handle the matter. The pig does not even agree to tell Ansula. "

"What is that?"

"He said, it will affect shooting. She's tense, but my baby is my important matter. "

"He's not going straight."

"I doubt it, Mr. Marthandan. He did not pick up the phone today. It is said that their team is shooting in Kuwait. But a while ago, Sandeep Kulkarni picked up the phone. In it I heard Thai music in the background. It's like a beach carnival going on nearby. "

"That means they're in Thailand."

"What if we locate their number?"

Jesse asked.

"We do not have the technology for that. Only the police can do that."

Ratheesh expressed helplessness.

Marthandan opened the suitcase and took out the laptop and put it on the table.

He turned it on and connected the internet modem.

A small box the size of a matchbox was connected via USB.

"This is a mobile tracker. Type of equipment used by detectives. It is not difficult for senior investigative journalists to use it. Please tell, what's the phone number of Ansula?

Marthandon said.

Ratheesh told Ansula's number.

The map appeared on the laptop screen.

Type the number in the search field

"That mobile is off. Tracking can only be done if the mobile is switched on.

Tell me the number of someone else on the team. Sandeep Kulkarni's or any team member of him "

Sandeep Kulkarni's number was also not available.

But he got Nicky's number.

Marthandon said.

"The location is Singapore itself. It is a suburban coastal area. They are camping in a hotel there. "

"Let's go there. It is wise to inform Ansula. "

Jesse said.

Marthandan zoomed in on the map location.

"This is a hotel called Paragonia. Where is the number that the kidnappers called in the morning?"

"I threw the phone away in anger. When it crashed, I took the SIM and put it in another phone. With that the number was gone. The latter did not call. "

"That's what they did. Don't they need Rs ten crore? What is the name of that woman? "

"Angel Toy."

Ratheesh said.

Marthanden searches Google for the name Porn star Angel Toy.

"Owner of a film production company called Phoenix Movies. Hollywood actress. Now settled in Paris. Why should they harm Ansula. What did those who called in the morning say? "

"He was harassed me and talked to a lot. He said, "I am a man who eats food that my wife commits adultery with."

When he said that, Ratheesh choked.

Marthandan closed his eyes and meditated.

And then said

"A Psychological Attack. They brutally reprimanded you. Unable to bear the grief, you threw the phone on the floor and smashed it. They never called after that. I'm sure. "

"That's correct"

"Naomi was kidnapped for some other reason. Let's do something. Let's find Ansula first. Let's go to Hotel Paragonia. "

Ratheesh came out in the same clothes he was wearing at home.

The three locked the apartment and drove into the city in Ratheesh's car.

Chapter 9

It was late at night.

It is about 30 km from there.

During the journey, Ratheesh got a call.

In pure American English.

The caller in the morning

"I think you're ready for a million dollars," he said. Did you advise your wife? It is not a pleasant arrangement to get fat by eating the food that the prostitute brings to many. "

Ratheesh was sweating when he heard such a phone conversation while driving. Because of the speaker, Jessie and Marthandan could hear it through the car's Bluetooth system.

Marthandan immediately turned on his laptop and set up the mobile tracker. He tracked the number that came on Ratheesh's phone now.

It turned out that the phone was in a moving vehicle.

The vehicle was traveling on the same route as they were going.

Marthandon also put his mobile number on the tracker.

They realized that the vehicle was following them.

Marthandan looked back.

A car follows.

There are two people in it.

Marthandan wrote in a paper:

"My people have come to arrange money. We have to wait till tomorrow morning. "

It showed Ratheesh.

He said it over the phone

Then the phone call was cut off.

"Now switch off your mobile phone."

Marthandon said.

Ratheesh did so.

Marthandan looked back.

"That car is right behind. They were waiting for Ratheesh to leave the apartment. This means that they are tracking Ratheesh's mobile. No more that fear. We will track them. For the time being, they do not know where we are going. Take the car to a hotel. "

Ratheesh drove his car to a nearby hotel.

There, he put the car in the parking lot and got off.

The car that came behind was seen pulling towards the roadside.

Marthandon said

"We do not have time. They will come here as Ratheesh's phone is not available on the tracker. Before that we have to go the other way through the back door of the restaurant. "

They did the same.

Reached the road on the other side and luckily they got a taxi.

"Hotel Paragania."

Marthandon suggested to the taxi driver.

"Isn't it near Lavana Beach where the carnival takes place?"

"Yes go fast."

Ratheesh said impatiently.

The car sped off.

Chapter 10

Ansula woke up half asleep.

The intoxication that had filled his nerves slowly began to subside.

The body began to feel pain as if it had been crushed.

There is pain and swelling in the genital area.

The shooting started at dawn.

One by one the men were enjoying themselves - as if in a relay.

Ansula rolled her eyes and looked around.

Nikki is looking at the mobile in the chair next to her.

There is no one else in the room.

When Ansula woke up, Nikki jumped up and started making syringes.

"No ... tell him to pack up."

Ansula suggested.

Nikki ignored it and filled the syringe with medicine.

Ansula was angry.

She lifted her legs and kicked Nicky's abdomen.

Nikki slammed into the corner of the room.

The syringe was thrown away on the floor from Nicky.

"You are my maid. Not the boss. "

Ansula stood up.

Her legs were sore.

She picked up the phone from the bag she had on the table.

Nikki jumped up and snatched the phone.

Ansula angrily took a flower pot from the table and slammed it into Nikki's head.

Nikki fainted and fell to the floor.

Ansula picked up the phone and went into the bathroom.

She turned on the phone which was switched off.

She called Ratheesh.

Ratheesh gave Ansula all the information.

Ansula was furious.

Her baby went missing in the morning.

Without saying that, Sandeep Kulkarni kept me injected drug and tortured all day.

I cannot forgive him for a second.

Hearing the noises in the room, Sandeep Kulkarni came inside.

Nikki was seen lying down.

He realized that Ansula was in the bathroom.

He knocked on the bathroom door

"Ansula, open the door."

"What is it?"

"Open the door."

"You're been using me since morning without even agreeing to urinate. Let me urinate in peace. You're gone for a while"

Ansula spoke to Sandeep Kulkarni in a language he had never used before.

"You speak too much."

He said angrily.

Ansula then filled a cup with boiling hot water.

"How can I talk to you, dog ...?"

Ansula asked and suddenly opened the door.

Sandeep Kulkarni, who was standing in front, poured hot water from the cup on his face.

He closed his eyes and sighed in pain.

Ansula picked up the camera tripod saw there and struck him.

Sandeep Kulkarni fell to the ground.

By then, two or three goons had run into the room.

Ansula saw a pistol tucked behind Sandeep Kulkarni's pants.

She pulled it out and pointed it at the goons.

"Get out now."

Ansula yelled.

The three of them came out.

Ansula locked the door of the room.

Then she put on her clothes.

Nikki and Sandeep Kulkarni were tied to the bed with a bed sheet.

Meanwhile, Ratheesh, Marthandan and Jesse came to the hotel.

Chapter 11

Ratheesh called Ansula.

Ansula said

"I have locked the room. That manager and two goons are out of the room. Do not leave them alone. Beware there will be weapons. "

Ratheesh and his gang had reached the hotel lobby.

The beautiful Mongolian receptionist accepted.

"What do you want, sir?"

"I want to see Sandeep Kulkarni. It is a visit. "

Marthandan said.

The receptionist looked at Jesse and passed out a false smile.

Marthandon pinched Jesse's thigh.

Receptionist Sandeep Kulkarni called on his phone.

Sandeep Kulkarni, who was lying unconscious, found his mobile phone in his coat pocket.

Ansula took it.

She saw the hotel number.

Said the receptionist as he answered the call

"Three people have come to see me."

Ansula said

"Leave them in the room."

"Yes madam."

The receptionist told Ratheesh and the group the room number and the floor.

They boarded the lift.

Ratheesh called Ansula.

"Ansula, you turn on that door cam and see where they are."

Ansula turned on the door cam.

It's a 180 degree camera.

The whole corridor was visible in camera.

You can see three people standing in front of the room.

Then Nikki woke up and cried.

Ansula ran and approached her.

Ansula slapped her on the arm.

Then he took the pistol and put it on Nikki's head.

"I will kill you."

"Please ... I can tell the truth. It was Sandeep who abducted Madam's baby. ”

Nikki said nervously.

"What ...?"

Ansula was shocked.

Unexpectedly, the truth fell out of Nikki's mouth.

Ansula angrily stabbed Nikki in the chin.

"Where is my baby?"

“The child is in the custody of the manager. The boy is still in the hotel. ”

Nicky said.

Ansula immediately informed Ratheesh over the phone.

Ansula approached the door, opened the door a little, put it in chains, turned around and hid.

"Where is my baby? I will kill your boss Sandeep, if you do not bring my daughter to me soon. Sure. "

"The baby is not in our hands."

The manager called from outside.

Of Ansula Anger doubled

"Nicky told me everything. It's all recorded. Concrete Evidence for the Police against You. I will not respond if my baby is released. Or.. "

Before she could finish, a pistol barrel reached through the door.

Ansula slammed the door hard before it the gun turned against her.

The hand holding the pistol suddenly slammed into the door and shattered.

In a fit of rage, the pistol exploded, shattering the cameras.

Ansula snatched the pistol.

She slammed the door shut and picked up the other pistol.

Ansula has never been shot with a pistol.

Now she does not know how to shoot, except pointing it out and screaming.

She aimed her pistol at Sandeep Kulkarni's leg and fired.

He was shot in the knee and screamed loudly.

Then the manager called out loud from outside the room.

"Do nothing to him. I will give the child. "

"Quick bastards, go and take the kid"

Ansula yelled.

Ansula saw through the door camera that the manager was giving instructions to two goons and they were running away.

Ansula called out.

"Manager, you kneel down. Take off your shirt and put it down. Put your weapons down. Do as you are told. "

She screamed as he stood motionless.

"I need to hurry."

When she realized that she was being watched, she did as she was told.

According to Ansula's phone call, Ratheesh and Marthandan, who were hiding in the corridor, ran and tied the manager to his shirt with his hands on the floor.

Then they turned and hid.

Ansula saw the goons appear in the corridor with the baby.

The goons only saw the manager.

Ansula opened the door and shouted.

"Hey, leave the baby in front and both of you take off your shirts and kneel down."

The goons stopped the walking.

The manager looked at them helplessly.

"Listen to what she said."

The two goons knelt on the ground and put their hands on their heads.

Ansula held out her pistol and slowly made her way down the corridor.

Ratheesh and Marthandan ran and tied the goons with their clothes.

Naomi ran over and hugged Ansula.

Ansula covered her with kisses.

She handed the baby to Jesse and went inside.

"I still have worked to do."

Later, Ratheesh and Marthandan went up to the room.

Ansula calmly asked as he sat next to Sandeep Kulkarni who was crying and shot him in the head.

"Why all this practice of yours?"

"Sorry...very sorry."

He cried.

Ansula suddenly kicked her gun into his face.

"Tell me, dog ... Why did you do this dirty work?" Didn't I just lie down like you said ... yet..? "

"I do this so that your husband and child would not interfere with your profession?"

"Hum what a profession ..."

Ansula spit.

Then he told Ratheesh and Marthandan.

"Hold on to this one."

Ansula lay down, took a syringe full of medicine and stabbed Sandeep Kulkarni in the body.

He cried.

Gradually he fainted.

"Take off his dresses."

Ratheesh and Marthandan started undressing Sandeep.

At that moment, Ansula heard something in the side room and looked at it.

Makeup artist Margaret was waking up after a deep sleep.

She was shocked to see all the scenes.

Ansula pointed her gun.

"Take off your dress."

Margaret shuddered in fear and took off her dress.

Sandeep, who was already naked, was lying on the bed.

Naked Margaret lay with him, and Nicky lay naked next to him.

"Two more to fuck him ... very clever."

Ansula sternly instructed both.

Then she picked up her mobile phone and started live on Face book.

Sandeep Kulkarni's nude sex filled the entire column with Face book Live.

Ansula had over 30 million followers on Face book in a short span of time.

Sandeep Kulkarni seems to be enjoying both the girls and closing his eyes.

Ansula came into the frame as it shattered in the background.

"I'm here to rip off the mask of a media terrorist. This is Sandeep Kulkarni. The owner of the Malayalam news channel News plus Seventeen, the world channel Big C News and the dodo phone channel Dodo Porn are having sex in front of you. I'm Ansula, the journalist who had to disguise herself as a prostitute to catch a horrible sex racket that has its roots all over the world. Yes, I am a journalist. I'm not a porn star. "

Ansula thus ended that fifteen minute long live.

By then, it had already garnered more than two and a half million viewers.

She put it straight on YouTube.

Shared on Twitter, LinkedIn and other media.

The whole world was shocked to see the video of Sandeep Kulkarni, a media terrorist.

News channels tried their best to hoard it but were unsuccessful.

Eventually, the wave of social media had to be taken over by the press, channel and media.

Ansula left the room satisfied.

Naomi jumped out of Jesse's lap and approached Ansula.

She took her daughter and walked away.

Ratheesh, Marthandan and Jesse followed.

The incident where a Malayalee woman journalist risked her life to trap a sex racket became news all over the world.

The world showered Ansula with congratulations.

www.ingramcontent.com/pod-product-compliance
Lightning Source LLC
Chambersburg PA
CBHW051451150726
48000CB00005B/2345